ANDY BRIGGS

WARRIOR NUMBER ONE

EDGE

From the author of HERO.COM and Tarzan: The Greystoke Legacy

Also by Andy Briggs:

The *Hero.com / Villain.net* series

Tarzan: The Greystoke Legacy

and in graphic novels:

Ritual
Kong: King of Skull Island

WARRIOR NUMBER ONE

Andy Briggs

EDGE
FRANKLIN WATTS

LONDON • SYDNEY

First published in 2011
by Franklin Watts

Text © Andy Briggs 2011
Cover design by Peter Scoulding

Franklin Watts
338 Euston Road
London NW1 3BH

Franklin Watts Australia
Level 17/207 Kent Street
Sydney, NSW 2000

A CIP catalogue record for this book
is available from the British Library.

Cover credit: Dark Geometry Studios/Shutterstock

ISBN: 978 1 4451 0707 3

1 3 5 7 9 10 8 6 4 2

Printed in Great Britain

Franklin Watts is a division of Hachette Children's Books,
an Hachette UK company.
www.hachette.co.uk

Chapter One

Twenty foes down, thirty to go.

The Warrior's blade sung through the air silencing his enemies. He vaulted over his victims as blood splattered the floor, their corpses piling high. He excelled in killing. Lucky blows from the evil hordes were easily deflected by the Warrior's blood-red armour.

More heads rolled as the Warrior pressed forward until only ten foul trolls remained, blocking the path into the city. With a roar, the Warrior charged, spilling the last vile drop of blood.

Bounding through the gates, the Warrior closed in on the Dark Lord...

★　★　★　★　★

Carl dropped the gamepad and cracked his knuckles. He admired his onscreen warrior as the body count appeared after completing the penultimate level of *Barbarianz*. The warrior was the ultimate digital creation. It had taken weeks and countless quests to get this far.

His mother shouted from downstairs. "Carl! Come and eat!"

Carl rolled his eyes. Didn't she understand that the next level would provide him with unimaginable power and worldwide respect?

"Carl! Now! Or I'll take that console off you!"

She had last wielded that dreaded threat when Carl used a rather creative swearword on his sister. He couldn't risk it happening again. He reached for the power button.

"Well done!" boomed a voice from the TV. "You are one step from liberating the world of Castellian from the threat of Dark Lord Greegan!"

"You are now..." the voice paused. Carl felt a thrill of apprehension. "Warrior Number Two!"

"Carl!" his mother screeched.

Chapter Two

Carl's mum had made one thing
clear – his console was off-limits until
tomorrow. So the rest of his Sunday
night was spent doing homework. His
mum had tried to get him to learn
extra things his teachers couldn't be
bothered teaching him, but he didn't
see the point.

Monday in school was grim as
usual. Carl felt pretty much alone; the
majority of his friends only existed as
names within *Barbarianz*, or as profiles
on Facebook. They were people Carl

had never met, but were the closest companions he had. They didn't judge him, and they were always there for advice. In real life few people wanted to talk to the four-eyed geek. He hated celebrity gossip, which alienated most people in school, and since all his conversations were geared around his adventures in *Barbarianz*, everybody else kept their distance. His skinny body and overuse of his asthma inhaler made sure he was the last to be selected for sports teams.

School dragged on as if time were passing through syrup. Finally, Carl experienced a burst of energy when the bell rang.

He ran home, inducing a fierce asthma attack, but it was worth it. He got home before anybody else, which meant at least an hour of uninterrupted gameplay.

He threw off his shoes, dumped his coat on the floor and sprinted upstairs to his room. *Barbarianz* loaded and had logged online by the time he sat down with a cool glass of cola. His palms were sweaty as he gripped the gamepad and his muscular Warrior avatar stepped through the city's gates.

His sword flashed, armour glinted and blood spilled. Tonight he was unstoppable. A hail of arrows turned the sky black but his magical shield easily deflected them. A row of hooded warrior-mages flung the darkest spells and hurled intense fireballs, but still the Warrior advanced, slaying them with lethal blows.

The Warrior pushed deeper into the city until he reached a wide plaza dominated by a five-headed dragon the size of a city block and breathing a quintet of destruction. It was Streebo and on his back rode the Dark Lord Greegan – the Warrior's final opponent.

Sunlight glinted from the Shadow Shard hanging around Streebo's middle neck. The opaque grey stone trapped an unstable cloud of dark energy: the source of all evil. Destroy that and the Dark Lord would be banished for ever.

Chapter Three

Carl blinked at the screen, his hands aching. He couldn't recall the past hour. What had happened?

"Congratulations," boomed the game. "You are now Warrior Number One!"

He couldn't remember how, but he had defeated the Dark Lord. He had achieved what nobody else in the world had done – he'd completed the game! Carl whooped like a maniac and threw his shirt over his head until he ran, painfully, into the open door.

"Warrior Number One! WHOOO!"

He felt complete exhilaration; the kind of success gold medal athletes must feel. He was Number One. The best in the world! No, the universe!

But who could he tell, other than his faceless-friends online? Who would hoist him onto their shoulders to celebrate?

No one.

That sucked.

★　★　★　★　★

A voice in the darkness woke Carl. His first thought was that he was dreaming or that he'd left on the TV. His hand groped for his glasses. Putting them on, he fumbled for the bedside lamp. It clicked uselessly. Had the bulb blown?

Then he noticed a very tall figure at the end of his bed, silhouetted by the streetlight outside. Must be his stupid sister.

"Do you know what time it is?" he mumbled.

"It is time to rise and meet your fate, Warrior!"

Carl sat bolt upright – that wasn't his sister unless something had seriously gone wrong. The voice sounded like the narrator from *Barbarianz*.

"W–who are you?"

As the darkness moved, Carl caught sight of a long cape that stretched into the TV screen.

"Folks call me the Sheriff. I've sought this world for you!"

Carl heard a horse whinny and, as his eyes adjusted, he could see the shape of a horse beneath the figure. Carl relaxed slightly; the animal confirmed that he must be dreaming. It would be impossible to get a horse up the stairs without his mum raising a fuss.

"Why me?"

"Are you not Warrior Number One?" Carl shoved his glasses back up his nose and nodded. "Then join me! Castellian has need of you! Rise, Warrior King!" boomed the man.

A cold leather glove snapped around Carl's hand and hoisted him onto the back of the horse.

The horse reared onto two legs. Carl threw his hands around the Sheriff's waist so he didn't slip off. The horse spun around and galloped towards the TV. Carl braced for impact — but instead his ears popped as the LED screen stretched like rubber and they passed through with a brief whiff of electrified air.

The horse's footfalls echoed as they passed through a tunnel. Seconds later they emerged, and Carl hiccupped in shock at what he saw—

They were in a sunlit vista of rolling forest-covered hills. Jagged snow-capped mountains crowned the horizon, mirrored in a huge lake that stretched to the foot of the trees.

The landscape passed in a blur. For several minutes the Sheriff said nothing. They trotted into an idyllic glade and the horse stooped to drink from a cascading waterfall. Carl took his cue to slide from its back. It was a long way down. Soft moss cushioned his landing, but he still managed to clumsily twist his ankle. The air was heavily scented and was rich with pollen, which triggered Carl's hay fever. How could this be a dream?

"Now, let me cast my eyes upon our hero!" boomed the Sheriff as he dismounted. Now in the daylight he stared at his new companion.

"By Thaigan's Beard, who are you?" the words tumbled from the Sheriff's mouth.

"Carl." He felt completely out of place in his pyjamas and was not sure what to say. He studied the old man.

The patchwork of leather armour across the Sheriff's chest was faded and marked with old tears and slashes. Dark eyes were fixed in a permanent squint beneath his bushy eyebrows and a knotted grey beard hung from his chin. He must have been in his fifties, his face weathered. He looked shocked.

"Impossible! How dare you impersonate Warrior Number One?"

"That's me! I did it!"

The Sheriff's entire body sagged. He staggered and sat on a fallen log, placing his head in his hands. "Aw, crud."

Chapter Four

"What were you expecting?" asked Carl defensively.

The Sheriff's gaze swept across him. "Muscles? Heroic stance? The build of an ox. Not..." he gestured limply, "this!"

Carl adjusted his glasses and wiped his nose on the sleeve of his pyjamas. "We're ruined," whimpered the Sheriff.

"No you're not. Look, this is my dream. I can do pretty much anything."

Carl spotted a broadsword strapped to the horse's flank. He slid it from the sheath and twirled it just as he'd done countless times in the game, but he wasn't expecting to feel the sword's weight and the steel spun from his grasp — thudding firmly into the ground between the Sheriff's legs.

The man sprung to his feet in alarm. "You moog! Watch what you're doing!"

"S-sorry," stammered Carl. Weight was something he'd never experienced in a dream before. He looked around the glade in fascination; how could this be real?

"You're sorry? My world is crumbling and dark days are upon us. You were our last chance. People thought I was foolish to trawl your world for a hero. I crafted the ultimate challenge to locate the finest warrior. You controlled a magical avatar that linked our worlds together. It re-enacted your every move within a magical reconstruction of Castellian. That's why it looked a little fake. It was a great idea, but sadly... you're the result." Again his head was in his hands. "I would be laughed from the Kingdom... if we were not all about to be mercilessly butchered. Well, at least I've got that to look forward to."

Carl felt an unfamiliar sense of pride swell within him, stoked by the Sheriff's harsh words.

"I did it controlling your avatar, how hard can it be for real?" He strained to pick the sword up. Bracing his feet, he managed to scythe it through the air. It would have looked dramatic if his pyjama pants hadn't chosen that moment to fall down.

The Sheriff's fingers parted from his eyes as he stared in horror at the boy. "You actually want to face the Dark Lord?"

Carl's cheeks burned with embarrassment as he pulled up his pyjama pants. He was fed up knowing he was Number One but being treated like Number Two.

"I passed the challenge, didn't I? I defeated the Dark Lord..."

"Fake Dark Lord."

"But it acted like the real one, right? I can do it again, even if this is a dream."

A flicker of a smile crossed the Sheriff's face. He admired the boy's

courage. "Or you can die trying!"
he cried, punching the air. That
wasn't Carl's plan, but the Sheriff was
suddenly animated again. "We need
to get you some proper clothes. Then
Dark Lord Greegan awaits!"

"What d'you mean, awaits? Don't
we go on a quest, do some intensive
training so I can build muscle? Learn
swordsmanship? Magic...?"

The Sheriff pointed at the sun. "Alas,
there is no time. High noon is the final
chance to kill the Dark Lord or we will
fall under his shadow for ever."

Carl yelped as the Sheriff suddenly
flicked his ear. "And this is no dream!
Come! To victory or death!"

Chapter Five

The city looked identical to the one in *Barbarianz*, except this version was real, with pointed blue roofs atop mighty towers reaching to the sky. Even from a distance, Carl could see guards on the ramparts looking out across a dark battlefield. It took a moment for him to realise that the blackness was actually the armour of half a million creatures that bore the Dark Lord's banners of a demon fist. He could smell their vile odour from here. That was something he'd never experienced in a game.

"Behold, the last city holding the darkness back."

Carl shifted uncomfortably. On their journey to the city, the Sheriff had patched together some mismatched armour, since nothing would fit Carl. He'd found him a horse too, although Carl didn't know how to ride it, thus becoming the first hero to be towed into battle.

Keeping out of sight, they approached the rear gates of the city and, with a sad sigh, the Sheriff gave his last advice.

"Keep your back straight. Hold your head high. At least you will die looking a little like a warrior."

That didn't comfort Carl. His eyes were streaming with hay fever and he couldn't see much through the smudges on his glasses.

The gates groaned open and they entered the city streets. Thousands of people lined the route, cheering and throwing rice in celebration. The wall of sound was deafening, but it didn't last long when the crowd finally saw their hero: a lanky kid in ill-fitting armour that revealed his blue pyjamas through the gaps. A deathly silence fell as the hopes of the city were abruptly crushed.

Carl waved half-heartedly. The Sheriff kept his gaze fixed ahead. He was so embarrassed, death might come as a relief. They stopped in a huge plaza – the one from *Barbarianz* where Carl's avatar had fought the Dark Lord.

The Sheriff looked at the crowd. "People of Castellian! After a long search and intensive selection process..." He could hardly believe his own words. "I bring you Warrior Number One. He who shall save us all!"

His voice echoed in the quiet street. A few people coughed. Somewhere chickens squabbled.

Carl felt something snap inside him. It was one thing to be treated as an outcast back home, but in this virtual magic realm he refused to be treated like a wimp. He drew his sword and raised it aloft with a quivering arm.

"Have I not proved myself as a champion? I will save you from the Dark Lord! I am your hero!" Carl was impressed with his conviction.

He almost sounded like a hero. "So where is Greegan?"

He was answered by a sudden flapping of leathery wings. A strong wind blew across the plaza as a giant shadow blotted out the sun. The crowd screamed and cowered. The Dark Lord was approaching!

Carl was only vaguely aware of the Sheriff galloping away from his side to join the terrified crowd, many of whom hid in the side streets. A massive five-headed dragon swooped overhead. The powerful downdraugh from its leathery wings overturned carts and blew Carl from his horse. The dragon landed, with one leg on a marble water fountain, which cracked under its weight. The ground trembled as the dragon settled down.

"Streebo..." muttered Carl. The last time he had encountered the dragon his bowels hadn't churned and his legs hadn't turned to mush. This was too real.

The dragon was impossibly huge. The rasping breath from all five heads sounded like mighty steam pistons and the stench was so overwhelming that Carl's nose went numb.

"Who dares challenge me?" roared a voice.

Carl looked around, unsure what to say. He saw the Sheriff, hiding under a cart, smiling feebly and giving Carl the thumbs up.

"Um... me!" stuttered Carl.

The five dragon heads peered at him, then bowed low. At first Carl thought – hoped – it was surrendering, but then he saw the unmistakable figure of Dark Lord Greegan on the creature's back. Greegan stepped down off one of the dragon's necks.

Carl gasped. Greegan was much taller than he remembered, standing twice Carl's height. His black armour was covered in spikes, tarnished by the blood of countless victims. His swarthy elfin features, pointed ears and a shock of white hair made him look terrifying.

Greegan peered down at Carl. "You? Surely you jest?" He looked at the frightened faces around him. "You have one chance to fulfil the prophecy. One chance to save your miserable land and this is your chosen hero? A puny, pitiful fool?"

The words evaporated Carl's fear.

He had defeated the Dark Lord once. It might have been a console game, but to Carl there was no difference. He raised his sword. The final moments of the game teased on the edge of his memory... what was it he had to do? His mind was racing, but his mouth was on a suicide mission of its own. He barely recognised his own voice.

"I am your downfall! I am Warrior Number One!"

He had hoped for a cheer from the crowd. Instead he received a wicked chuckle from Greegan as he drew his scimitar. The blade erupted into flames. Carl could feel the heat on his face.

"We shall see, Warrior!" Greegan spat. "When the clock strikes twelve – you die!"

He pointed to a clock tower from which hung a mighty bronze bell. Even as Carl watched, a clockwork hammer drew back and struck it.

BONG! Carl's eyes darted around. How had he defeated the Dark Lord in the game? Something about a shard...

BONG! Greegan sneered at Carl.

BONG! Carl cut the air with his blade. At best he might give Greegan a nasty bruise before he was slaughtered.

BONG! Carl scanned the faces of the townsfolk. All hope had left them.

BONG! The Shadow Shard... Carl was so lost in thought that he didn't hear the next two chimes. The Shard contained unstable dark energy – the source of Greegan's power! In the game he had somehow destroyed the Shard—

BONG! Carl squared up to Greegan, his eyes searching for any sign of the Shard. Surely, he must keep it close? He couldn't see anything.

BONG!

"You will die slowly, Warrior," Greegan taunted. "My army will consume this world – then your own!"

BONG! Carl tried to remember. The Shard... It was... his eyes caught a flicker of sunlight from something hanging around the dragon's middle neck. It was the Shard.

How was he supposed to get it?

Then the answer came to him. Greegan was waiting for the final chimes, but Carl would strike now!

Chapter Six

Before the eleventh chime struck, Carl charged with a roar – catching the Dark Lord off guard. Greegan spun around and swung his flaming scimitar—

He missed as Carl slid between the Dark Lord's legs, sprung to his feet and ran towards Streebo.

All the dragon's heads were still lowered. It hadn't expected the small warrior to jump suddenly onto its central head. Carl brought his sword down with every ounce of strength he possessed.

The blade bounced off the thick scales with such force that the sword jolted from his hands. He suddenly remembered that Streebo was impervious even to metal.

That was a problem.

The dragon roared and bucked – all the heads quickly straightening up.

"Whoa!" Carl lost his balance and slid down the scaly neck. He would have fallen if he hadn't snagged the heavy chain holding the Shadow Shard in place. His feet pedalled in the air – the ground now far below. He suddenly realised how stupid he had been, the chain was too thick to hack apart.

How had he destroyed the Shard in the game?

"Kill him!" screamed Greegan.

The middle head tried to shake Carl off, but he held on with grim determination. The four other heads reared back – they all had the same idea.

Carl felt the fierce intake of air as the mighty dragon breathed in. Four jaws opened, revealing jagged teeth the size of kitchen knives. The air ignited at the back of each throat in balls of radiant multicoloured flame.

Then he suddenly remembered the move that had earned him Warrior Number One status.

Carl let go of the chain. It was

perfect timing, honed by the many hours he'd invested in playing *Barbarianz*. He fell just as the four dragon heads unleashed super-heated torrents of fire on the fifth.

"NNNOOO!!" Greegan's screams were drowned out as Streebo's fifth head exploded. The Shadow Shard shattered under the pressure. The unstable darkness it contained was released in a violent pressure wave that tore the dragon apart.

Greegan dropped to his knees – but exploded into ash before he hit the ground. The blast wave roared through the surrounding streets like a hurricane. It burst through the city gates and washed across the battlefield, turning Greegan's minions into slime as it wiped the valley of evil.

For a whole minute, all that could be heard was the splatter of fried dragon meat as it rained down across the plaza. The crowd slowly emerged, searching for their hero. There was no sign of him.

Then he emerged from under a smashed market stall. It was Carl, bruised, singed and covered in dragon guts. His hand groped for his glasses. Amazingly they hadn't broken. Putting them on brought the crowd into focus. Every mouth was open; every eye wide.

The stunned Sheriff approached Carl.

"What happened?" asked Carl groggily. His ears were ringing from the deafening explosion and his eyebrows were missing.

"The Warrior has saved us all!" screamed the Sheriff, triumphantly lifting Carl's arm.

The crowd surged forwards, lifting Carl onto their shoulders and a million people cheered.

"Carl! Carl! CARL!"

A smile crept across Carl's face. One so intense he wondered if it would ever go. Maybe he should never leave Castellian? This place suddenly felt more like home; after all, he had already spent many weeks exploring it.

Here, he was a hero.

Here, he was Warrior Number One.

About the author

Andy started writing on movie projects such as *JUDGE DREDD* and *FREDDY VS JASON* and *FOREVERMAN* for Spiderman creator Stan Lee, and legendary film producer Robert Evans.

WARRIOR NUMBER ONE is Andy's 10th book. If you like superheroes and action adventure then you can read his *HERO.COM* or *VILLAIN.NET* series.

Or, if you think swinging through the jungle and fighting rebel soldiers is more fun, then check out Andy's reboot of the 100-year-old character, Tarzan, with the thrilling *TARZAN: THE GREYSTOKE LEGACY* and *TARZAN: JUNGLE WARRIOR* (published summer 2012).

You can find out more exciting news on Andy's website:

www.andybriggs.co.uk

or follow him on Facebook:
www.facebook.com/andy.briggs1
or Twitter: twitter.com/abriggswriter

One mermaid's journey
to find her mother

Katherine Langrish

forsaken

EDGE

"Langrish is a first-rate
storyteller" The Times

Turn over to read an extract from
forsaken:

The current tugged through the room. I could sense the tide turning. My family would soon be home. Every day since she left, they followed the high tide far into the bay, calling "Mama!" from the tops of the tumbling breakers – their thin voices like seagulls crying. Not me. I'd had enough of waiting and calling.

I tucked the baby back in the seashell cradle as it rocked gently in the sea sway, anchoring him into his harness of ribbon-weed. I dropped a kiss on his forehead. Then with a slash of my tail I rode the current out of the window. I was furious, with Father as well as with Mama. What was the good of crying and calling from the breakers? How was she ever going to hear? It was pointless: it was feeble.

If I wanted Mama back, I would have to go and fetch her.

I put my arms together over my head and shot upwards. The rugged pinnacles of Father's palace dropped away. I swam fast; I didn't want the others to see me. I whirled through rosy clouds of krill, through a shoal of herring that divided and sprayed around me like a silver fountain. I left the blue deeps, aiming for the round, crinkled, shifting lid that was the light of the world above. Suddenly the water was full of dazzling bubbles. I felt the swells catch and throw me. My head splashed out into the air.

This is just the start of Mara's journey. To find out if she finds her mother, get hold of a copy of Forsaken today!

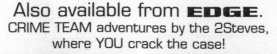

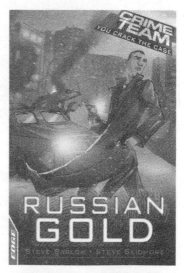